Sherlock Holmes and The Lamplighter's Mystery

Mabel Swift

Sherlock Holmes and The Lamplighter's Mystery

(A Sherlock Holmes Mystery - Book 5)

By

Mabel Swift

Copyright 2024 by Mabel Swift

www.mabelswift.com

All rights reserved. No part of this publication may be reproduced in any form, electronically or mechanically without permission from the author.

This is a work of fiction and any resemblance to any person living or dead is purely coincidental.

Contents

Chapter 1	1
Chapter 2	7
Chapter 3	14
Chapter 4	19
Chapter 5	25
Chapter 6	32
Chapter 7	36
Chapter 8	41
Chapter 9	45
Chapter 10	48
Chapter 11	51
Chapter 12	56
Sherlock Holmes and The Vanishing Act - first two chapters	64

The Sherlock Holmes series	78
A note from the author	80

Chapter 1

The rain pattered against the windows of 221B Baker Street, the sound a gentle accompaniment to the crackling fire in the hearth. Sherlock Holmes sat in his armchair, long fingers steepled beneath his chin, his grey eyes fixed on some distant point. Dr John Watson, as was his habit, busied himself with the day's newspaper, occasionally tutting at some article or another.

A sharp knock at the door roused both men from their respective reveries. Mrs Hudson, Holmes's long-suffering landlady, entered, her expression one of mild apology. "A Mr Percy Wentworth to see you, Mr Holmes. He seems quite distressed."

Holmes straightened, a glint of interest in his eye. "Send him in, Mrs Hudson."

Moments later, a man entered the room. He was in his early fifties, with a lean, agile frame that spoke of a life of physical labour. His clothes, though well-worn, were clean and neatly patched. He removed his cap, twisting it nervously in his hands.

"Mr Holmes, Dr Watson," he began, "I apologise for the intrusion, but I didn't know where else to turn."

Watson gestured to a chair. "Please, sit down, Mr Wentworth. Tell us what troubles you."

Wentworth sat, perching on the edge of the seat. "It's my job, sirs. I've been a lamplighter for nigh on thirty years, and I've never had a problem like this before."

Holmes leaned forward, his attention fully captured. "Go on."

"Someone's been sabotaging my work," Wentworth said, his hands clenching around his cap. "Lamps that I know I've lit, they're out again when I check on them later. And my tools, they go missing, or I find them broken. I'm falling behind on my rounds, and I'm afraid I'll lose my job."

Watson frowned. "Have you reported this to your superiors?"

Wentworth shook his head miserably. "What can I tell them? That I'm suddenly incapable of doing the job I've done for decades? They'll think I've gone mad, or that I'm too old for the work."

Holmes steepled his fingers once more. "You mentioned 'someone'. Have you seen this person?"

Wentworth hesitated, then nodded. "A few times, I've spotted a figure lurking in the shadows. Always at night, always when I'm on my rounds. But when they realise I've seen them, they run off. I've never got a clear look at them."

The detective's eyes narrowed. "And this, combined with the sabotage, has led to your current state of distress?"

"I haven't slept in days," Wentworth admitted. "I'm jumping at every shadow, expecting to see that figure. And the thought of losing my job, well, it's too much."

Watson, his face etched with sympathy, turned to his friend. "Holmes, surely we can help?"

Holmes was silent for a few moments, his gaze distant. Finally, he said, "Mr Wentworth, we will take your case. I cannot abide a mystery, and this one presents several intriguing points. The identity of your shadowy stalker, and the motive behind the sabotage. Yes, this is something we can help you with."

Relief washed over Wentworth's face. "Thank you, Mr Holmes. Thank you."

Holmes said, "Mr Wentworth, we will need more details about your work. Your nightly rounds, your duties, anything that might shed light on this mystery."

Wentworth nodded, a glimmer of pride entering his eyes as he spoke of his profession. "Of course. As a lamplighter, it's my job to ensure the gas lamps in my assigned area are lit at dusk and extinguished at dawn. I'm responsible for maintaining the lamps, too. Cleaning the glass, replacing the mantles, and making sure there's enough gas. It's not an easy job, sirs. We're out in all weathers, and the hours are long. But there's a satisfaction in it, knowing you're helping to keep the city safe and bright."

Watson, ever the empathetic listener, nodded. "I can imagine. And your rounds, Mr Wentworth? Do you follow the same route each night?"

Wentworth sat up a little straighter. "Yes, Dr Watson. I'm responsible for the lamps around the Downing Street area. Those streets are where many government offices are situated, and some people inside them work all hours, sometimes into the night. It's imperative that the lamps are in good working order. I've been doing that area for ten years now. It's one of the most important rounds in London. I know of many lamplighters who would love to be in charge of those lamps. Which makes this sabotage business even worse. I don't want to lose that round, not when I've worked so hard to make it mine."

"And your colleagues, your supervisors, what do they think of your work?" Holmes asked.

A touch of colour appeared in Wentworth's cheeks. "Well, I don't like to boast, Mr Holmes, but I'm well-respected in the company. I've always been diligent, you see. Never missed a shift, never had a complaint. I take pride in my work, and I think that shows. And I always make sure my record book is up to date. It's where I make notes about my rounds. The times when I lit and extinguished the lamps, and any repairs I had to make, that sort of thing. My record book is my most important possession and I take great care of it. My supervisors are always impressed with how efficient I am at keeping detailed notes." He fidgeted with his cap, his gaze dropping to the floor. "That's why this business has me so rattled. I can't bear the thought of them thinking I'm slipping, that I can't do my job anymore."

Watson reached out, patting Wentworth's shoulder reassuringly. "We understand, Mr Wentworth. And we'll do everything we can to get to the bottom of this."

Holmes, meanwhile, had risen and was pacing the room, his brow furrowed in thought. "The tools of your trade, Mr Wentworth, where do you store them when you're not using them?"

Wentworth blinked, surprised by the question. "In the alley behind my lodgings. There's a storage area at the end of it. It's where some of the other lamplighters keep their equipment, too. I keep my toolbox there, and my ladders as well."

Holmes nodded, a glint in his eye. "I see. And have you noticed anything unusual there? Any signs of disturbance or tampering?"

Wentworth frowned, thinking. "Now that I know of. My ladder is always where I leave it. And my toolbox too. Unless I've missed something obvious."

Holmes said, "It is possible that in your tired state, you may, indeed, have missed something. Perhaps some vital clue that the shadowy saboteur has left behind. This gives us a starting point. Mr Wentworth, I will need the address of your lodgings, and your permission to examine the storage area."

Wentworth, looking somewhat bewildered, nodded. "Of course, Mr Holmes. Anything you need. As it happens, I'm heading back home now."

"Excellent!" Holmes declared. "Then we shall come with you and start our investigation immediately. We will have your mystery cleared up in no time at all, Mr Wentworth."

Chapter 2

As the trio walked through the bustling streets of London, Percy Wentworth led the way, his shoulders hunched against the drizzling rain. Sherlock Holmes and Dr John Watson followed close behind.

After a brisk ten-minute walk, they arrived at a narrow, nondescript building tucked away in a side street.

"This is it," Wentworth said, gesturing towards a wooden door. "My lodgings."

He led them down a cramped alley that ran alongside the building. The space was barely wide enough for two people to walk abreast; the cobblestones slick with rain and grime. At the end of the alley, they came to a small, walled-off area.

"This is where we keep our equipment," Wentworth explained as he opened the door to the area.

Holmes stepped into the storage area, taking in every detail of the scene. It was cluttered with various tools and implements, such as ladders, toolboxes, coils of rope, and spare lantern parts. A low brick wall enclosed the space, but it would have been easy enough for someone to climb over, especially under the cover of darkness.

Watson, too, was examining the scene with a critical eye. "It doesn't seem very secure," he commented. "Anyone could access this area, especially if the door is left unlocked, as it was now."

Wentworth said, "There's never any need to lock it. We trust each other." He paused. "Or we used to, but I'm starting to think otherwise now, what with my damaged and lost tools."

Holmes crouched down, running his fingers over the ground. "There are several sets of footprints here. Difficult to distinguish with the rain, but it's clear this area sees regular traffic." Rising, he said, "Your ladder, Mr Wentworth. Which one is it?"

Wentworth pointed to a tall wooden ladder leaning against the wall.

Holmes approached it, running his hands over the rungs and examining the joints. "No obvious signs of damage or tampering," he said after a moment. "Now, where is your toolbox? I can see several here."

Wentworth said, "I keep mine tucked behind my ladder."

"Ah, yes, I see." Holmes examined the battered toolbox, which was locked. "Again, there are no signs of tampering. But that doesn't mean much. A clever saboteur would know how to cover their tracks. I assume your toolbox is always kept locked?"

Wentworth nodded. "It is." He gave them a wry smile. "But it's not the best of locks. I've had it for years and I think it's more rust than metal now."

Holmes shot him a smile. "Perhaps it's time for a new lock. Could we see your room? And the records you mentioned?"

Wentworth led them back out of the alley and into the building. They climbed a narrow, creaking staircase to the third floor, where he unlocked a door and ushered Holmes and Watson into a small, sparsely furnished room.

"It's not much," the lamplighter said apologetically, "but it's home."

Watson looked around, taking in the narrow bed, the washstand, the small table and chair. A single window looked out over the rooftops of London. It was a humble abode, but clean and well-kept.

Wentworth went to the table and picked up a leather-bound book. "These are my records," he said, handing it to Holmes. "Every lamp I've lit, every repair I've made, it's all in here. My route details are in it, too."

Holmes flipped through the pages, his eyes scanning the neat, precise entries. "You keep very detailed accounts, Mr Wentworth."

A hint of pride entered Percy's voice. "I have to. The Lamplighter's Office requires it. We have to submit our records every month for review."

Watson frowned. "And what happens if there are discrepancies? If a lamplighter falls behind on their duties?"

Percy's face darkened. "It's not good, Dr Watson. The Lamplighter's Office takes a very dim view of any failings. If a lamplighter isn't doing their job properly, they can be dismissed. And that's not all I have to worry about. I'm a member of The Lamplighter's Union, and they send inspectors around to check on our records, sometimes without any warning. And if the inspectors find anything amiss, they'll let the Lamplighter's Office know. Again, it could be a reason for dismissal."

Holmes handed the book back to Wentworth. "Now, if you could walk us through your nightly routine. Every detail, if you please. The more we know, the better equipped we'll be to unravel this mystery."

"Of course, Mr Holmes. It all starts when I arrive at the yard to collect my equipment. I make a note of what time I do that. Let me show you." Wentworth flipped through the pages of his record book. His eyes suddenly widened in disbelief. "This isn't right! Someone has been in my room, tampering with my records! Look, you can see how they've made it look as if I left for work later than I did, and that I returned too early. This isn't right at all! If an inspector turns up to look at this book without any warning, I'll be in real trouble, that's for sure."

Holmes walked slowly around the room. He examined the door and windows, searching for any signs of forced entry, but found none. The lock on the door was old but sturdy, and the windows were latched from the inside.

"No obvious signs of a break-in," he said, his brow furrowed in thought. "Which suggests that whoever did this either had a key or was let in. Mr Wentworth, I need you to think carefully. Is there anyone who might have a grudge against you? Another lamplighter, perhaps, someone who lives in this building or nearby?"

Wentworth hesitated for a few moments before saying, "Well, there's Horace Cuthbert. He's been a lamplighter for about ten years. He's always arguing with everyone, often for no reason at all. A real grumpy sort, and selfish too. And Horace has been after my route for years. He's made no secret of that. I get the feeling he's also jealous of how well-liked I am at the company."

Holmes nodded. "And where does Mr Cuthbert live?"

"Just down the street," Wentworth replied. "But surely it couldn't be him? I mean, Horace is a difficult man, but to go this far?"

Holmes held up a hand. "We must not rule out any possibilities, Mr Wentworth. Jealousy and resentment can drive men to desperate acts. We need to approach this carefully. If Mr Cuthbert is indeed behind this, we will need proof. Solid, irrefutable proof."

Watson added, "And we must act quickly. If those altered records are seen by someone in an official capacity by one of those inspectors you mentioned, well..." He didn't need to finish the sentence. The consequences hung heavy in the air.

Wentworth slumped down onto his bed, his face pale. "What am I going to do? I don't want to lose my job. It means the world to me."

Holmes turned to face the distressed lamplighter. "You're not going to lose your job, Mr Wentworth. I give you my word. We will solve this mystery. And soon. Do you have Mr Cuthbert's address?"

Wentworth said, "I do. He'll be starting his rounds soon. Shall I give you those details as well?"

"Please," Watson said.

Once they had the required information, Holmes said, "We will take our leave, Mr Wentworth, but we will be in touch soon." He tipped his hat in farewell and left the room with Watson at his side.

Chapter 3

Armed with the details of Horace Cuthbert's round, Holmes and Watson walked through the darkening streets of London.

The rain had lessened to a fine mist, but the chill in the air was palpable. As they walked, they noticed the lamplighters at work, their ladders propped against the lampposts, the soft glow of the gas lamps gradually illuminating the city.

"It's a thankless job," Watson mused, pulling his coat tighter around him. "Out in all weathers, ensuring the streets are lit for the rest of us."

Holmes nodded. "Indeed, Watson. And yet, for men like Percy Wentworth, it's a matter of pride. A job well done, a city kept safe."

Sometime later, they turned a corner onto the route that Cuthbert covered and heard a voice grumbling loudly. Following the sound, they soon came upon a man at the top of a ladder, his face twisted in a scowl as he worked on a lamp.

"Blasted rain," he muttered, his voice carrying down to the street below. "Freezing my fingers off up here. And for what? A pittance of pay."

Holmes and Watson exchanged a glance. This could only be Horace Cuthbert.

They waited patiently as the man descended the ladder, his movements stiff and jerky, whether from the cold or his own ill temper, it was hard to say. As he reached the ground, Holmes stepped forward.

"Mr Cuthbert, I presume?" he said, his voice pleasant but firm.

Cuthbert's eyes narrowed suspiciously. "Who's asking?"

"My name is Sherlock Holmes, and this is my associate, Dr Watson. We have an interest in the work of lamplighters and were hoping to have a word with you about your profession."

Cuthbert snorted, gathering up his tools. "What about it? I do my job, same as any other."

Watson spoke, "We've heard good things about your work, Mr Cuthbert. Your round takes you quite far afield, doesn't it?"

For a moment, the man's face softened, a glimmer of pride shining through. "That it does. All the way from here to the river, and back again. It's a long night's work, but I get it done."

Holmes nodded, his expression one of interest. "And what of your fellow lamplighters? We've heard that Percy Wentworth, in particular, has a rather coveted route."

At the mention of Wentworth's name, Cuthbert's face darkened, a sneer twisting his lips. "Wentworth? Ha! He's had it easy for years, with that cushy route of his. He's got much shorter distances than me. And lower lamps. It's a wonder he even needs a ladder! I'll be glad when he retires, I will. I've already put my name down for his round. It's about time someone else had a chance at an easy night's work."

Holmes studied the man. Cuthbert's resentment was clear, but was it enough to drive him to sabotage?

"I know who you are!" Cuthbert suddenly exclaimed, his voice laced with suspicion. "You're that detective, aren't you? I've seen your picture in the papers."

Holmes remained impassive, his expression giving nothing away. "My reputation precedes me, it seems."

Cuthbert sneered. "I get it now. It must be Wentworth who's been in touch with you, then. What's he been saying? Spinning some yarn about someone messing with his work? And pointing the finger at me?"

Holmes replied, "I'm afraid I cannot confirm or deny any client's business, Mr Cuthbert. I'm sure you understand."

Cuthbert let out a nasty laugh, shaking his head. "Oh, I understand all right. I heard Wentworth muttering about sabotage at the last Lamplighter's Union meeting. Load of old nonsense, that's what it is. Seems like he's seeing and hearing things, if you ask me. A sure sign he needs to hang up his ladder and retire, before he causes problems for the rest of us."

Watson frowned. "Problems? What do you mean?"

Cuthbert shrugged. "Well, if a lamplighter's not right in the head, who knows what could happen? He could miss a lamp, or he might not check the gas pipes properly and cause a leak. It's a matter of public safety, isn't it? Perhaps I should let one of the inspectors at the Union know about Percy's state of mind. They'd want to know if one of their lamplighters was losing his grip. Yeah, that's what I'll do. And I'll do it soon." He reached for his ladder. "Anyway, I've got work to do. Lamps won't light themselves, will they?"

With that, Horace Cuthbert turned on his heel and strode off into the misty night, leaving Holmes and Watson standing in the flickering light of the gas lamps.

Watson turned to Holmes. "Do you think there's any truth to what he's saying, Holmes? Could Mr Wentworth be imagining things?"

Holmes was silent for a moment, his eyes following Cuthbert's retreating figure. "It's possible. The mind can play tricks, especially under stress. But I'm not ready to dismiss Mr Wentworth's concerns just yet. There's more to this than meets the eye, I'm sure of it. But even so, we should speak to Mr Wentworth again now. Warn him about Mr Cuthbert's threat so he can prepare himself should an inspector turn up at his home. I have committed Mr Wentworth's route to memory from the information I saw in his record book. Let's head in that direction forthwith. Time is of the essence."

Chapter 4

As the evening settled over London, Holmes and Watson made their way through the winding streets, arriving at the trail of lit lamps that marked Wentworth's route. The flickering gas light cast an eerie glow, the shadows seeming to dance and twist with each step they took.

Up ahead, they spotted Wentworth using his long pole to ignite one of the lower lamps. His movements were practised and efficient, the result of years of experience.

But just as Holmes and Watson were about to approach him, a flicker of movement caught Holmes's eye. It came from one of the narrow alleyways that branched off the main street, a shadowy figure lurking almost out of sight.

Without a word, Holmes' hand shot out, grasping Watson's arm and pulling him into the shadows. They pressed themselves against the cold brick wall, their breath misting in the chill air as they watched the scene unfold before them.

The figure stepped out of the alleyway, their features obscured by the darkness. They seemed to be watching Wentworth intently.

Suddenly, as if sensing the eyes upon him, Wentworth spun around, his gaze locking onto the mysterious figure.

"Oi!" he yelled, his voice ringing out in the quiet street. "What do you think you're doing, lurking about like that?"

The figure startled, clearly not expecting to be spotted. In a flash, they darted back into the alleyway, their footsteps echoing off the cobblestones.

Holmes and Watson were in motion instantly, springing from their hiding place and giving chase. They raced down the alleyway, their coats billowing behind them as they ran.

The figure was fast, weaving through the labyrinth of side streets and back alleys with a clear familiarity. Holmes and Watson pursued, their breath coming in sharp gasps as they pushed themselves to keep up.

"Quickly, Watson!" Holmes called out, his voice tight with exertion. "We mustn't lose him!"

They turned a corner, expecting to see the figure ahead, but the alley was empty. They skidded to a halt, their eyes scanning the shadows for any sign of movement.

"Blast!" Holmes hissed, his frustration evident. "He's given us the slip."

Watson leaned against the wall, trying to catch his breath. "Who do you think he was, Holmes? Did you get a good look at him?"

Holmes shook his head, his brow furrowed in thought. "I didn't. But it's likely the person who is behind this sabotage business. Come, Watson. We must return to Mr Wentworth. He saw us take up the chase, and he'll want to know if we captured anyone."

Wentworth was waiting for them when they emerged from the alleyway, his face etched with worry.

"What happened?" he asked. "I saw you chasing after that man. Did you catch him?"

Holmes shook his head. "Unfortunately not. He knows these streets too well, it seems."

Wentworth's shoulders slumped, a look of defeat in his eyes. "So what now? Am I to spend every night looking over my shoulder, wondering when he'll strike again?"

Watson said, "We won't let that happen. Holmes and I are on the case now. We'll unmask that man, I guarantee you." He shared a look with Holmes before continuing. "I'm afraid we have some bad news for you. We spoke to Horace Cuthbert, and he's threatening to report you to an inspector at the Lamplighter's Union. Mr Cuthbert is going to claim that you are losing your mind, and that you could be a threat to public safety."

Wentworth paled. "He would do that? Then I'll lose my job for sure. There's going to be a meeting tomorrow morning at ten. I expect he'll do it then." He cast a wistful glance at the lit light above him. "This could be the last time I light these lamps."

Holmes said, "Don't give up hope yet, Mr Wentworth. It would be wise for Watson and myself to attend that meeting. It may give us an opportunity to speak with the other lamplighters and determine if anyone else has been the victim of sabotage. Then you'll know you're not the only one. May we have the address of where the meeting will take place?"

"Of course," Wentworth said, and he gave them the address.

Holmes took out his notebook and jotted down the information. "Excellent. Watson and I shall be there."

Watson, sensing the unease that still lingered in the lamplighter's demeanour, said, "Mr Wentworth, if it would make you feel more at ease, I could accompany you for the remainder of your rounds tonight."

Wentworth's face brightened at the offer. "That would be most appreciated, Dr Watson. Thank you."

Holmes nodded his approval. "A fine idea, Watson. I shall leave you to it and meet you back at Baker Street later."

As Holmes departed, Watson fell into step beside Wentworth, the two men making their way through the gas-lit streets of London. The rain had finally ceased, and the clouds parted to reveal a sky filled with glittering stars.

Around them, the city was settling in for the night. Families gathered in the warm glow of their homes, the sound of laughter and conversation drifting through open windows. Shopkeepers pulled down their shutters, securing their wares for the evening.

Wentworth moved from lamp to lamp. Watson watched, impressed by the man's dedication to his craft. Despite the weight of the situation bearing down on him, the man never faltered, ensuring that each lamp was lit and functioning properly.

As they walked, Watson engaged Wentworth in conversation, hoping to distract him from his worries. They spoke of their respective professions, the challenges they faced, and the satisfaction they derived from a job well done.

Time seemed to fly by, and before long, they had reached the end of Wentworth's route.

The lamplighter turned to Watson, gratitude shining in his eyes. "Thank you, Dr Watson. Your company has been a great comfort tonight."

Watson clapped a hand on Wentworth's shoulder, offering a reassuring smile. "Think nothing of it. Holmes and I will see you tomorrow at the Union meeting. I know this is a worrying time for you, but if you can, try to get a good night's sleep."

With a nod, Wentworth bid Watson goodnight and disappeared into the shadows, heading for home. Watson watched him go, a sense of determination filling his heart. Poor man. They would not let him lose his beloved job.

Chapter 5

Just before ten the next morning, Holmes and Watson arrived at the Lamplighter's Union building, a sturdy brick structure with large windows that allowed the morning light to filter through. They stepped inside, their eyes adjusting to the dimmer interior. The room was filled with the murmur of conversation as lamplighters gathered, some standing in small groups, while others took their seats at the long wooden tables that filled the space.

They made their way further into the room. Holmes's keen gaze swept over the assembled people, taking in every detail. He nudged Watson and inclined his head towards a corner where Horace Cuthbert stood, deep in conversation with another man.

"Let us move closer, Watson," Holmes said, "but discreetly. I believe their discussion may prove enlightening."

The two men casually made their way towards Cuthbert. As they drew nearer, Cuthbert's agitated voice reached their ears.

"It's not right, I tell you," Cuthbert hissed. "Percy's too old for the job. He's making mistakes. He's putting lives at risk. It's time for him to step aside and let someone else take over. Someone like me."

The other man, whom Holmes assumed was one of the union officials going by his smart attire, shook his head. "Now Horace, you know it doesn't work like that. Percy's still doing a fine job, and he hasn't given any indication that he's ready to retire."

Cuthbert's eyes narrowed. "But you promised me his round. You said it would be mine."

The official sighed, his patience clearly wearing thin. "I said no such thing. And even if Percy were to retire, his round wouldn't automatically go to you."

"What?" Cuthbert spluttered, his face reddening. "Then who would get it?"

"If Percy doesn't retire, his round will likely go to Miriam Reeves," the official said, his tone firm. "She's been doing an excellent job, especially considering she's only been a lamplighter for less than a year."

Cuthbert looked like he was about to argue, his mouth opening and closing like a fish out of water. But before he could speak, a bell rang out, signalling the start of the meeting.

As the lamplighters began to take their seats, Holmes and Watson spotted Percy Wentworth entering the room. They caught his eye and gave him a discreet nod, which he returned with a grateful smile.

Holmes and Watson found seats near the back of the room.

Holmes leaned close to Watson, his voice low. "It seems our friend Horace Cuthbert is not above using underhanded means to get what he wants," he said, his attention fixed on the disgruntled lamplighter a few rows ahead.

Once the last lamplighters had settled into their seats, the man who had been conversing with Cuthbert earlier took his place at the front of the room.

The man's voice carried easily through the room. "For any of those who don't know me, I'm Rupert Blackmore, the senior inspector with the Union. Thank you for turning up to this meeting. Now, let us begin."

Blackmore proceeded to cover the usual topics expected at such a meeting, discussing the importance of maintaining the lamps and ensuring they remained lit throughout the night. However, he also brought up a few complaints from some members of the public, which caused a stir in the seated lamplighters.

"It has come to our attention that some lights went out hours after they were lit," Blackmore said, his brow furrowed. "Unfortunately, it caused some people to lose their footing on the dark paths, and I regret to say, minor injuries were sustained."

A voice interrupted the meeting. It was Cuthbert, who stood up and demanded, "Whose round was it? Who's responsible for this negligence?"

Blackmore fixed Cuthbert with a stern gaze. "It is a private matter, Mr Cuthbert, and one that I will be discussing with the individual in question soon."

Cuthbert turned his head, sought Percy Wentworth, and gave him a pointed look. With a self-satisfied smirk, he sat back down.

The meeting concluded shortly after, and the lamplighters dispersed. Holmes and Watson, who had been observing the proceedings with keen interest, noticed Blackmore approaching Percy Wentworth. In perfect unison, Holmes and Watson stood and took a few steps closer to them.

They overheard Blackmore speaking in a low, concerned tone. "Percy, I'm afraid it was the lamps on your round that went out. This is highly unusual, especially considering your exemplary record. Is everything alright?"

Wentworth looked embarrassed. "I'm not sure what to make of it, Mr Blackmore. I always check them. I am so sorry this has happened, I really am."

Blackmore sighed. "I'm concerned, Percy. Not only about the lamps but also about some rumours I've heard regarding your state of mind. I fear for your well-being and your future employment if this continues."

"I assure you, Mr Blackmore, I'm perfectly fine. There must be some mistake. I'll double my efforts and ensure this never happens again," Wentworth said with as much confidence as he could muster.

Holmes and Watson watched as Blackmore walked away, leaving Wentworth standing alone, his face a picture of misery.

The two men approached their client.

"Mr Wentworth," Holmes said, "we are still investigating this matter thoroughly. We will find the culprit behind these troubling events. We overheard a conversation between Horace Cuthbert and Mr Blackmore before the meeting started." He gave Wentworth the details of that conversation.

Wentworth said, "I'm not that surprised, especially after you told me about his threat yesterday. I was half-hoping he wouldn't go ahead with it."

"And what of this Miriam Reeves that Mr Blackmore mentioned?" Holmes asked.

Wentworth's face softened at the mention of Miriam's name. "Ah, Miriam. She's a lovely young woman, one of the few female lamplighters in our area. I had the pleasure of training her when she first started, almost a year ago now."

Watson raised an eyebrow. "And how has she been performing in her role?"

"Oh, she's a quick learner, that one," Wentworth said, a hint of pride in his voice. "Keen to do well and always willing to put in the extra effort. She's been given a round near mine recently, and I've seen her checking the lamps multiple times throughout the night."

Holmes said, "Mr Wentworth, do you think it's possible that Miriam could be behind the sabotage?"

Wentworth shook his head vehemently. "No, no, I don't believe so. Miriam is a hard worker and has always been friendly and supportive. I can't imagine her doing something like this."

Holmes nodded, his expression pensive. "I understand your perspective, Mr Wentworth, but we must consider all possibilities. Could you provide us with the details of Miriam's round? We would like to speak with her, just to gather more information."

Wentworth hesitated for a moment, then nodded. "Of course, Mr Holmes. I'll write down the streets she covers and the times she usually starts and ends her shift."

Chapter 6

As the afternoon waned and darkness began to fall, Holmes and Watson headed through the misty streets of London, their steps purposeful as they sought Miriam Reeves. The gas lamps flickered to life one by one, casting an eerie glow across the cobblestones as the lamplighters began their nightly rounds.

They found Miss Reeves atop a ladder, her nimble fingers adjusting the wick of a lamp. She glanced down at the approaching figures, a flicker of recognition in her eyes.

"Mr Holmes, Dr Watson," she called out. "I saw you at the meeting this morning. I had a feeling I might see you again soon."

Holmes tipped his hat in greeting. "Miss Reeves, I presume. Might we have a word?"

She nodded, descending the ladder with ease. "Of course. I suspect this is about Percy and the trouble he's been having."

Watson said, "You've heard about the sabotage, then?"

"I have," Miss Reeves replied, her expression grave. "Percy's been talking to me about it for weeks now. He's convinced someone's out to get him, messing with his lamps and watching him from the shadows."

Holmes's eyes narrowed. "And what do you make of these claims?"

She sighed, her gaze drifting to the darkening streets. "At first, I thought it might just be his mind playing tricks on him. The night can do that, you know, especially when the fog rolls in. But I've experienced something, too. A shadowy figure, lurking in the alleys. Watching me as I work. Every time I shout at them, they disappear into the night."

"This is most concerning," Holmes said. "Miss Reeves, if Mr Wentworth were to retire, would his round be assigned to you?"

"I couldn't say, Mr Holmes. It would be an honour to take on his route, I can't deny that. But I wouldn't want Percy to retire, not because he thinks someone is out to get him."

Holmes said, "Do you have any suspicions about who might be behind these troubles?"

She shook her head. "I don't. I know Horace Cuthbert wants Percy's round. He's always going on about it. But I don't think he'd stoop so low. But there again, no one really knows another person, do they? Not really." She sighed heavily. "I hope you find out who is responsible. Percy's a good man, and he doesn't deserve this."

Watson said, "We are looking into this matter, and are sure we'll uncover the truth."

Miss Reeves smiled. "That's good to know. If you don't mind, I have to get back to my work."

Holmes and Watson bid Miss Reeves farewell and walked away.

A few minutes later, Holmes said, "Do you think she could be lying, Watson? It's possible that Miss Reeves is the one sabotaging Mr Wentworth's work."

Watson glanced at his companion. "But why would she do such a thing?"

Holmes replied, "She stands to gain from it. It's a coveted position, and one she clearly desires."

Watson nodded slowly, mulling over Holmes's words. "That may be true, but what about the shadowy figure we saw? Miss Reeves mentioned seeing it too."

"Ah, yes," Holmes said. "We saw a figure lurking in the shadows, but we assumed it was a man. However, you no doubt noticed Miss Reeves is dressed in trousers and a coat, not unlike a man's attire. In the darkness, it would be easy to mistake her for a male figure."

"Ah, yes, I see. And because she was trained by Mr Wentworth, she would be familiar with his tools and his record book, and where they are kept. If it is Miss Reeves, I wonder how she got into his room."

"Hmm, that's something we will find out in due course. It does trouble me that Miss Reeves could be behind this, considering how highly she thinks about Mr Wentworth. However, that could be an act. I suspect there is something we are missing; some truth yet to be revealed."

Watson said, "So what do we do now, Holmes?"

The detective's eyes gleamed with a familiar intensity. "We continue our investigation. If Miss Reeves is involved, we will uncover her deception."

Chapter 7

Inside 221B Baker Street the next morning, Holmes and Watson were deep in conversation when Mrs Hudson ushered in Percy Wentworth, who was in a highly distraught state. Mrs Hudson gave Holmes and Watson a swift nod before quickly leaving the room.

"Mr Holmes, Dr Watson," Wentworth began. "Something terrible has happened."

Holmes was on his feet in an instant. "What is it, Mr Wentworth?"

"It's my ladder. I think someone is trying to murder me. Could you come to my lodgings? It'll be easier to show you what's happened."

Without a word, Holmes grabbed his coat and hat, motioning for Watson to follow. The three men hurried through the streets of London and made their way to Wentworth's lodgings.

Once there, Wentworth led them to the storage area. With shaking hands, he pointed to his ladder, which lay propped against the wall.

Holmes and Watson examined the ladder, their eyes widening as they saw a deep, jagged cut that ran partway through the wood. It was clear that someone had deliberately sawn through the ladder, weakening it to the point of danger.

"I noticed it this morning. I came in here to check my toolbox and to see if anything was missing. I took your advice, Mr Holmes, and got a new look. My tools are all still there. I noticed that cut in that ladder when I was putting my toolbox back into its usual place. If I hadn't noticed it before my shift, I could have fallen and broken my neck. And I'm sure that shadowy figure has been following me more. I thought I saw him on the way to your home."

Holmes examined the ladder with a critical eye. "It's extremely fortunate that you noticed this cut, Mr Wentworth."

"That's not all, Mr Holmes. My record book, it's gone."

Holmes looked up from the ladder. "Gone? When did you last see it?"

"Last night, when I came home from my shift. I was so tired when I came in that I thought I might have put it somewhere else to keep it safe. I convinced myself I had, and that I would find it in the morning. But when I woke up and had a good look in every place possible, it was nowhere to be found."

Holmes suggested they have a look for any signs of forced entry to his room. After a thorough search, there wasn't any evidence of any illegal entry. The window was securely latched, and the door showed no signs of tampering. Holmes discreetly looked for the record book, in case Mr Wentworth, in his tired state, had missed it.

After their fruitless search, Wentworth said, "I don't know what to do. Without my record book, I'm finished. I might as well retire now and save myself the shame of being dismissed."

Holmes said kindly, "Nonsense, Mr Wentworth. We will not let this saboteur win. Watson and I will do everything in our power to find the culprit and clear your name."

"But I can't work without my ladder."

Holmes waved a dismissive hand. "Leave that to me. I have a neighbour, Ernest, who has a ladder. I'm certain he will be more than willing to lend it to you for the time being."

Wentworth's shoulders sagged with relief. "Thank you, Mr Holmes. I don't know what I would do without your help."

"We will sort this out, Mr Wentworth," Holmes said. "I promise you that. Now, let me go and speak with Ernest about that ladder."

Leaving Watson behind to offer comfort to Mr Wentworth, Holmes hastened back to Baker Street, where he immediately set about procuring a ladder from their neighbour, Ernest. The kind-hearted man was more than happy to lend his ladder to the distressed lamplighter. Holmes wasted no time in returning to Wentworth's abode.

Wentworth's face lit up with gratitude as he saw Holmes approaching with the ladder in tow. "Oh, Mr Holmes, I can't thank you enough," he exclaimed. "You've saved my livelihood, you have."

Holmes replied, "Think nothing of it, Mr Wentworth. We're happy to help in any way we can."

But even as Wentworth took the ladder and leaned it carefully against the wall, a shadow of worry crossed his face. "But what about my record book? I can't work without it. The union inspectors, they'll have my head if I don't have my records in order."

Watson, ever the practical one, reached into his coat pocket and pulled out a small, leather-bound notebook. "Here," he said. "This is a new journal that I popped into my pocket this morning in case I needed it. Your need is much greater than mine, Mr Wentworth. Besides, I have many more empty journals at home. You can use it to record your rounds for now, and then transfer the information to your official record book once we find it."

"Dr Watson, I don't know what to say. Thank you, truly." Wentworth gave him a smile.

Holmes said, "Try to keep your spirits up, Mr Wentworth. We'll find your record book, and we'll catch the scoundrel who's trying to sabotage you. You have my word on that."

Chapter 8

After leaving Wentworth's home, Holmes suggested to Watson they speak with Mr Blackmore about the relationship between Percy Wentworth, Horace Cuthbert and Miriam Reeves.

Holmes said, "Mr Blackmore knows these people better than us, and he may have some important information that will help our investigation."

Watson nodded in agreement, and together they returned to the Lamplighter's Union building and went inside. As they made their way down the hallway towards the offices, a movement caught Holmes' eye.

There, in one of the offices, was a furtive-looking Horace Cuthbert. He appeared to be rifling through some papers on the desk, his movements quick and nervous. As soon as he noticed Holmes and Watson, his face darkened, and he quickly rushed out of the office.

"Mr Cuthbert!" Holmes called out, his voice sharp. "What were you doing in that office?"

Cuthbert snarled, his eyes narrowing. "It's none of your business, Mr Holmes. Now, if you'll excuse me."

With that, he pushed past the two men and ran down the hallway, disappearing around a corner. Holmes and Watson exchanged a puzzled glance, but before they could pursue the matter further, a voice called out from behind them.

"Mr Holmes, Dr Watson! What a surprise to see you here."

They turned to see Mr Blackmore walking towards them, holding two steaming cups of tea.

Blackmore said, "I noticed you at our meeting the other day and was going to ask what your interest in lamplighters was, but alas, I never got the chance. Union business never stops." He looked into the office where Cuthbert had been, a frown creasing his brow. "That's odd. Mr Cuthbert was just here a few minutes ago, asking to speak with me about his promotion prospects. But it seems he's changed his mind."

Holmes said, "Mr Blackmore, we were hoping to speak with you about Percy Wentworth. As you may know, he's been experiencing some troubling incidents as of late."

Blackmore nodded. "Yes, I've heard. It's a terrible business, truly. Percy is one of our best lamplighters, and it pains me to see him going through such difficulties." He gestured for Holmes and Watson to follow him into his office. He set the cups of tea down on his desk and moved some papers to the side. "Please, have a seat. I'll tell you everything I know."

Holmes and Watson sat down, and Holmes asked if Blackmore could tell them about Mr Wentworth.

Blackmore said, "Percy has been with us for many, many years. He's always been a reliable and hardworking employee. I've never had any complaints about his work, and he's always been diligent about keeping his records in order."

Holmes asked, "And what about Mr Cuthbert and Miss Reeves? What can you tell us about them?"

Blackmore sighed, shaking his head. "Horace Cuthbert is a bit of a troublemaker, I'm afraid. He's been with us for about ten years now, but he's always been more interested in advancing his own position than in doing his job well. He's been angling for Percy's route for some time now, but I've made it clear that it will go to Miriam Reeves if Percy retires."

Watson said, "And how has Miriam been performing in her role?"

Blackmore's face lit up with a smile. "Oh, she's been a revelation. She's only been with us for about a year, but she's already proven herself to be one of our most promising lamplighters. She's hardworking, reliable, and has a keen eye for detail. I have no doubt that she'll go far in this profession."

"And have you noticed anything unusual in the past few weeks?" Holmes asked, "Any strange occurrences or suspicious behaviour?"

Blackmore shook his head. "Apart from Percy's lamps going out unexpectedly, nothing out of the ordinary, I'm afraid. But I'll keep my eyes and ears open, and let you know if I hear anything."

With that, Holmes and Watson thanked Blackmore for his time and took their leave. As they stepped out into the cool evening air, Holmes turned to Watson with a determined look in his eye.

"We're getting closer, Watson," he said. "I can feel it. We just need to keep digging, and we'll find the truth behind this mystery."

Chapter 9

Holmes and Watson stepped out of the Lamplighter's Union building and walked away.

Holmes suddenly stopped, his attention focused on the tall grass at the side of the path.

"What is it, Holmes?" Watson asked, looking in the same direction.

Without a word, Holmes strode over to the grass and reached down, his long fingers closing around a familiar object. As he held it up to the fading light, Watson gasped in recognition.

"Why, that's Mr Wentworth's record book!" he exclaimed, his eyes wide with surprise.

Holmes nodded, his expression grim as he examined the book. It was intact, but the cover was slightly damaged, as if it had been dropped or handled roughly.

"Indeed, Watson," he said. "And I suspect Mr Cuthbert may have had something to do with this."

Watson asked, "But why would Mr Cuthbert take that record book? And why would he drop it here, of all places?"

Holmes turned the book over in his hands. "It's possible he dropped it by accident on his way to see Mr Blackmore. Or perhaps he left it here on purpose, knowing Mr Wentworth would be unable to perform his duties without it."

"The scoundrel," Watson said with a shake of his head. "Speaking of Mr Cuthbert, what was he looking at in Mr Blackmore's office? And why would he run away when we confronted him?"

Holmes tucked the record book into his coat pocket. "I don't know. But I intend to find out. First, however, we must return this book to Mr Wentworth. Later, we will seek out Mr Cuthbert and speak to him again. Let's see if he's more forthcoming with information this time."

They set off walking again.

Watson said, "And what of Miss Reeves? Do you think she could be involved in any way?"

Holmes shook his head. "I doubt it, Watson. From what Mr Blackmore said, she seems to be an exemplary employee. But we can't rule anything out at this stage."

As they turned the corner onto Wentworth's street, they saw the lamplighter coming out of his building. His face lit up when he saw Holmes and Watson.

"Mr Holmes, Dr Watson!" he cried out. "Have you any news for me?"

Holmes reached into his pocket and withdrew the record book, holding it out with a small smile. "We found this, Mr Wentworth," he said. "Someone may have taken it from your lodgings and dropped it outside the Lamplighter's Union building."

Wentworth took the book. "Oh, thank you, Mr Holmes. I'm so relieved to have it in my hands again. But who could have taken it? And why?"

Holmes replied, "We have some suspicions. But we need to gather more evidence before we can make any accusations. In the meantime, I suggest you keep a close eye on your belongings and report any further incidents to us immediately."

Wentworth nodded. "I will, Mr Holmes. And thank you again, both of you."

After assuring Wentworth they would be in touch with him again soon, Holmes and Watson took their leave and headed back to Baker Street.

Chapter 10

Later on, as the sun began to set, Holmes and Watson set out in search of Cuthbert once more. They navigated the winding alleys and narrow passages, their footsteps echoing in the growing darkness. The air was thick with the scent of smoke and the distant sounds of the city settling in for the night.

As they approached the streets where Cuthbert conducted his rounds, they noticed the lamps were already lit, casting a warm glow across the pavement. They pressed on, their eyes scanning the streets for any sign of the lamplighter.

At last, they spotted him up ahead, perched on his ladder as he prepared to light the next lamp. But just as he reached for the wick, a shadowy figure emerged from the darkness and rushed towards the ladder.

Before Holmes or Watson could shout a warning, the figure purposely collided with the ladder, sending it toppling to the side. Cuthbert let out a cry of surprise as he tumbled from his perch, landing hard on the unforgiving stone below.

The shadowy figure darted away, disappearing into the night as quickly as they had appeared. Holmes and Watson raced towards the fallen lamplighter.

Watson reached Cuthbert first, kneeling beside him to assess his injuries. The lamplighter was unconscious, a nasty gash on his forehead oozing blood onto the pavement. Watson quickly checked his pulse and breathing, relieved to find both steady, if a bit weak.

"He's suffered a nasty blow to the head," Watson reported. "We need to get him to a hospital immediately."

Holmes nodded. "I'll go after the attacker," he said, already turning to give chase. "You stay with Cuthbert and summon a cab."

Watson nodded, watching as Holmes disappeared into the shadows in pursuit of the mysterious figure. He turned his attention back to Cuthbert, using his handkerchief to apply pressure to the wound on his head.

It wasn't long before Holmes returned, his expression frustrated and his breathing heavy from the chase. "They got away, yet again," he said, his voice tight with anger.

Watson said, "There's a cab waiting for us over there. Help me get Mr Cuthbert into it."

Together, they managed to place Cuthbert into the back of the cab. Watson got in with him.

Holmes said, "We can't leave Mr Cuthbert's ladder and equipment unattended. I'll take them to the storage area behind Mr Wentworth's house. With a bit of luck, I might catch sight of that shadowy figure on the way."

"This is getting more serious by the minute," Watson said. "First the sabotage, then the stolen record book, and now this attack on Mr Cuthbert. What could be the motive behind all of this?"

Holmes shook his head. "I don't know, Watson," he admitted. "Our priority at this moment is Mr Cuthbert's health. Let's not waste any more time. Get him to the hospital. We'll meet later."

With that, the cab clattered away through the darkened streets.

Holmes watched it go, feeling an annoying sense of frustration about the case. He hoped the mystery could be solved before anyone else was hurt.

Chapter 11

Next morning, Holmes and Watson sipped their tea as they discussed the events of the previous night. The attack on Cuthbert had left them both shaken and more determined than ever to uncover the truth behind the sabotage of the lamplighters.

"It's a dreadful business," Watson said, shaking his head. "Who could have pushed Mr Cuthbert off his ladder like that? And why? Could it have been Miss Reeves after all?"

Holmes replied, "I still don't believe Miriam Reeves is behind this. She has no motive to go after Mr Cuthbert, and from what we've seen of her, she seems to be a diligent and honest worker."

Watson nodded, taking another sip of his tea. "But who could it be? And what do they hope to gain by sabotaging the lamplighters?"

"That, my dear Watson, is the question we must answer," Holmes replied. "But there is one curious detail that may provide a clue. You mentioned Mr Cuthbert was mumbling something in his hospital bed last night?"

Watson sat up straighter, his eyes widening with realisation. "Yes, that's right! He kept repeating 'the Electric Illumination Company' over and over again before he fell asleep. I couldn't make any sense of it."

Holmes said, "I have read in the papers about plans to replace the gaslights with electric ones in certain parts of the city. It's possible that someone from the electric company might be behind these attacks, perhaps in an effort to prove the superiority of electric lighting over gas."

Watson frowned, considering the idea. "But why target the lamplighters specifically? Surely there are other ways to promote the benefits of electric lighting without resorting to sabotage and violence."

"Perhaps," Holmes mused, his fingers drumming on the arm of his chair. "But we must not discount any possibilities at this stage. I think it would be wise for us to pay a visit to the Electric Illumination Company and find out more about their plans. We need to determine how the introduction of electric lighting could affect the local lamplighters and their livelihoods."

Watson set down his teacup. "I agree. We should go at once. We don't want anyone else to get hurt."

The two men quickly gathered their coats and hats and stepped out into the bustling streets of London.

Holmes and Watson soon reached the gleaming new offices of the Electric Illumination Company. The building stood out amongst its neighbours, its exterior adorned with sleek, modern lines and large windows that allowed the bright glow of electric light to spill out onto the street.

The interior of the building was no less impressive, with polished marble floors and walls lined with the latest in electrical technology. Electric lamps cast a steady, unwavering light, banishing the shadows that so often lurked in the corners of gas-lit rooms.

The reception desk was manned by a young woman with a neat, efficient air about her.

"Good afternoon, gentlemen," she said, looking up from her work with a polite smile. "How may I assist you today?"

Holmes removed his hat and inclined his head in greeting. "Good afternoon, miss. My name is Sherlock Holmes, and this is Dr Watson. We were hoping to speak with someone about the company's plans for installing electric lights in the city."

The receptionist nodded, consulting a ledger on her desk. "Certainly, Mr Holmes. Mr Ranger would be the best person to speak with regarding that matter. However, he is currently in a meeting. Would you be willing to wait?"

"Of course," Holmes replied, and he and Watson took their seats in the waiting area.

As they sat, Holmes noted the way the electric lamps cast a steady, unwavering light, so different from the flickering glow of gas. He observed the people coming and going, their faces illuminated by the bright, modern lighting.

Suddenly, a familiar figure caught his eye. Descending the stairs was none other than Mr Blackmore, the inspector from the Lamplighter's Union. He was deep in conversation with another man, their faces animated as they spoke. The two men seemed on friendly terms, laughing and smiling as they reached the bottom of the stairs.

Holmes watched as Mr Blackmore shook hands with his companion, a broad grin on his face. The inspector seemed in high spirits, completely unaware of Holmes and Watson's presence in the lobby. With a nod, Mr Blackmore turned and strode away, leaving his companion to head in the opposite direction.

Holmes turned to Watson, his brow furrowed in thought. "Did you see that, Watson?" he murmured, keeping his voice low to avoid being overheard.

Watson nodded, his own expression one of surprise. "What could Mr Blackmore be doing here, at the electric company? And who was that man he was speaking with?"

"I don't know," Holmes replied. "But I intend to find out."

A short while later, Mr Ranger approached them. It was the same man who had been speaking with Mr Blackmore.

Mr Ranger greeted them warmly and asked, "Can I help you with something, gentlemen?"

Holmes stood, an eager look in his eyes. "You most certainly can, Mr Ranger. We have some questions for you."

Chapter 12

Holmes and Watson returned to the Lamplighter's Union building the very next day. They entered the meeting room and were greeted by Mr Blackmore, who looked at them with a mixture of curiosity and apprehension.

"Mr Holmes, Dr Watson," he said, shaking their hands firmly. "I must admit, I'm rather intrigued by your request to call this emergency meeting. What exactly do you plan to say to the members?"

Holmes gave him an enigmatic smile. "All will be revealed in due course, Mr Blackmore. Suffice it to say, it has something to do with a recent investigation of ours."

Mr Blackmore raised an eyebrow but said nothing further. As the members of the Lamplighter's Union filed into the room, he took his seat at the front.

The room buzzed with conversation as the lamplighters took their seats, their faces a mixture of confusion and curiosity. Percy Wentworth sat near the front, his face pale and drawn, while Miriam Reeves and a few others cast worried glances in his direction.

When everyone had settled, Holmes addressed the seated people, his voice clear and commanding. "Thank you all for coming on such short notice," he began. "I know you must be wondering why we've called this meeting. As some of you may know, my associate Dr Watson and I have been investigating a series of troubling incidents involving members of your union. Specifically, we have been looking into the case of Mr Percy Wentworth, who has been the victim of what appears to be a campaign of sabotage and intimidation."

Wentworth shifted uncomfortably in his seat as people looked his way.

Holmes continued, "Mr Wentworth has been an exemplary member of this union for many years, and yet someone has seen fit to target him, to undermine his work and threaten his livelihood. And he is not the only one. Just two days ago, Mr Horace Cuthbert was the victim of a vicious attack. He was forced off his ladder and seriously injured."

The room erupted in gasps and exclamations.

Holmes held up a hand for silence, and the room gradually quieted. "Thankfully, Mr Cuthbert is recovering in hospital. At first, Dr Watson and I believed these attacks might be motivated by jealousy or greed. After all, the position of a lamplighter is a coveted one, and there are those who might go to great lengths to secure a more favourable route or a higher standing within the union. But as we delved deeper into the case, we began to suspect that something else was at play. Something far more insidious than mere personal ambition."

The room was deathly silent now, everyone's attention fixed on Holmes as he spoke.

Holmes turned to face Mr Blackmore and said, "We believe the attacks on Mr Wentworth and Mr Cuthbert were not the work of a jealous colleague or a disgruntled rival. No, we believe they were part of a larger conspiracy, one that threatens the very future of lamplighters." He paused, letting his words sink in. "Mr Blackmore, would you care to explain to the members of this union why Dr Watson and I saw you shaking hands with Mr Ranger, a manager at the Electric Illumination Company, yesterday?"

Blackmore's face paled, and he shifted uncomfortably in his seat. "I... I don't know what you're talking about, Mr

Holmes. I've never met anyone from the electric company."

But Holmes was not to be deterred. "Come now, Mr Blackmore. We spoke with Mr Ranger himself, and he confirmed he had offered you a job at the electric company. A job which, I might add, you have accepted."

Cries of disbelief and anger rang out. Wentworth looked stunned, his eyes wide with shock.

Holmes pressed on, his voice rising above the din. "But that's not all, is it, Mr Blackmore? You see, we believe you have been deliberately sabotaging Mr Wentworth's lamps and his tools, to prove how unreliable human lamplighters can be."

Blackmore folded his arms. "You can't prove anything, Mr Holmes. This is all just wild speculation."

But Holmes was not finished. "Oh, but we can prove it, Mr Blackmore. You see, you chose Mr Wentworth's route for a very specific reason. It's the route that covers the streets where many of London's most influential politicians live. And you knew that if the lamps on those streets started going out, the politicians would take notice. They would question the reliability of the lamplighters, and would start to look for alternatives. Alternatives like electric lighting. And they are in a position to make changes happen quickly."

The room was silent now, every eye fixed on Blackmore. He looked around wildly, his face a mask of desperation and anger.

"But you didn't count on Mr Cuthbert finding out about your little scheme, did you?" Holmes continued. "He saw the documents in your office, the ones that proved you were planning to work with the electric company. And that's why you pushed him off his ladder. To keep him quiet. Perhaps quiet forever."

Blackmore said, "Okay! I admit it! But I did what I had to do for the future of this city. Electric lighting is the way forward, and the lamplighters are nothing but a relic of the past. They need to be replaced, and I was just doing my part to make that happen. And getting a job at that company secures my future."

Wentworth stood up, his face red with fury. "You traitor!" he shouted. "How could you do this to us? We trusted you!"

But Blackmore just sneered at him. "Trust? What good is trust in a world that's moving on without you? The future belongs to those who embrace progress, not those who cling to the past."

Holmes said, "And what about the lamplighters you have hurt, Mr Blackmore? Are they just collateral damage in your grand plan for progress?"

Mr Blackmore's face twisted into a mocking smile. "Progress always has its price, Mr Holmes. And if a few people have to suffer along the way, well, that's just the way it is."

His words caused people to leap from their seats and yell insults at Blackmore, a man they had trusted for years.

Holmes nodded to a couple of police officers at the back of the room who entered unobserved, especially by Mr Blackmore.

Holmes looked directly at Blackmore and said, "Your treachery has been exposed. There's no coming back from it. You won't be heading towards a bright future with the electric company. The only place you're going to is prison." The corners of his mouth twitched. "Which, at the present time, is completely illuminated by gas lamps."

The police led Blackmore away. The stunned lamplighters stood up and gathered in groups to discuss the shocking revelations.

Wentworth approached Holmes and Watson. "I can't believe it. I just can't. Mr Blackmore, of all people." He shook his head in disbelief. "Mr Homes, Dr Watson, thank you, for everything. I'll never forget what you've done for me. And for the other lamplighters as well. One thing still troubles me, though. How did Mr Blackmore get into my room without breaking in?"

Holmes said, "Knowing you would be on your rounds, Mr Blackmore visited your lodgings and spoke to your landlord. He claimed you had given him permission to enter your room at any time. The landlord had met Mr Blackmore frequently when he'd visited you and other lamplighters in the building, so he wasn't the least bit suspicious and let him in. After hearing the truth about Mr Blackmore, your landlord said he will never make that mistake again. He was most upset about what had happened."

"Ah, I see. That explains it. It wasn't my landlord's fault. He trusted Mr Blackmore. We all did." Wentworth sighed softly. "Well, I'd better get ready for my shift tonight. I'll call on Horace at the hospital first. See how he is, let him know what's happened. Thank you again, Mr Holmes, Dr Watson, you've saved my job. And my sanity."

Percy Wentworth walked away, looking much brighter and with his head held high.

"So, that's that," Watson said. "Holmes, do you think the gas lights of London will be replaced with electric ones?"

"It's highly likely," Holmes said. "The world is constantly evolving. Progress and innovation can't be stopped. But who knows, maybe some of those beautiful lamps will survive and cast their glow upon the people of the future, perhaps people even a hundred years from now."

Watson chuckled. "You're getting almost poetic, Holmes. May I say, even emotional?"

Holmes laughed. "It will soon pass. Come, Watson, I can sense there is another mystery waiting for us."

***

Read on for the first two chapters in the next book: Sherlock Holmes and The Vanishing Act

Sherlock Holmes and The Vanishing Act - first two chapters

Chapter 1

A knock sounded at the door of 221B Baker Street, echoing through the cluttered sitting room where Sherlock Holmes sat in his armchair, pipe in hand, lost in thought. The door creaked open and Mrs Hudson poked her head in.

"Mr Holmes, there's a young woman here to see you. She says it's urgent."

Holmes straightened up. "Show her in, Mrs Hudson."

The landlady nodded and stepped aside, ushering in a petite woman with chestnut curls and brown eyes. The woman's cheeks were flushed and her eyes red-rimmed, evidence of recent tears. She clutched a lace handkerchief in her hands.

"Thank you, Mrs Hudson," Holmes said, rising to his feet.

Mrs Hudson gave the distraught young woman a sympathetic look before withdrawing, closing the door softly behind her.

Holmes gestured to the settee. "Please, have a seat Miss...?"

"Meyer. Mrs Lily Meyer," the woman said, dabbing at her eyes. "I've come about my husband, Alex. He's gone missing, Mr Holmes. Vanished without a trace."

Dr Watson, who had been sitting quietly in the corner, lowered his newspaper and said gently, "When did this happen, Mrs Meyer?"

The woman replied, "Last night. Alex is a street magician. He performs regularly in an East End courtyard. He always draws a big crowd. People love him." She gave Watson a small smile. "But he didn't come home last night. I haven't slept, waiting for him to return."

Holmes steepled his fingers under his chin. "Has his disappearance got something to do with his performance?"

"Yes, Mr Holmes, it was his final trick that somehow went wrong," Mrs Meyer explained, twisting the handkerchief in her hands. "For that final trick, Alex's assistant would tie him up in chains and ropes, then lock him inside a large trunk. Seconds later, Alex would jump out of the trunk, free from the ropes and chains."

"Only this time, I take it, your husband did not reappear from the trunk?" Holmes asked.

Mrs Meyer shook her head, fresh tears welling in her eyes. "That's right. And when his assistant opened the trunk, Alex wasn't there. He had vanished. He's not been seen since."

Watson made a small noise of sympathy. "How awful for you, Mrs Meyer. To have your husband disappear like that, it must be quite a shock."

"It's not like Alex to simply abandon a performance," Mrs Meyer said. "Something must have happened to him, something dreadful. And he always comes home after his show without fail. We've never spent a night apart since the day we got married. I'm so worried about him. What could have happened?"

"Tell me more about your husband's career as a street magician," Holmes said. "Who does he associate with in the course of his work?"

Mrs Meyer answered, "Alex has become more and more popular over the last year, and he always has a large crowd watching him, most of them from the East End. I have noticed some more well-off people attending, too." She hesitated for a few moments. "I think his popularity may have earned him some enemies among the other street magicians."

Watson asked, "What do you mean, Mrs Meyer?"

"Alex's usual spot in the courtyard is prime territory. It's sheltered from the wind and has good visibility from the surrounding buildings. Some of the other magicians have been known to grumble about him monopolising the best pitch."

Holmes nodded. "I see. And have any of these disgruntled performers made threats against your husband?"

Mrs Meyer shook her head. "Not that I know of. Alex tends to keep such things from me because he doesn't want me to worry. But there have been times, when I've gone to watch Alex's show, when I've heard mutterings from some people in the crowd. Comments about him being too flashy, too eager to please the toffs in the audience."

"And did you ever see who was making these remarks?" Holmes asked.

"No. The courtyard is always packed during Alex's performances, and I'm usually too busy watching him to look around me. Even after all this time, I can't take my eyes off Alex when he's performing. He's mesmerising."

Holmes said, "It's possible, then, that your husband may have run afoul of a jealous rival, someone seeking to eliminate the competition by nefarious means."

Mrs Meyer gasped at Holmes' words.

Watson said gently, "Have you reported your husband's disappearance to the police?"

Mrs Meyer's eyes filled with fresh tears. "I tried. As soon as I realised Alex was truly missing and not just delayed, I went to the local station house. But the constable on duty just laughed at me. He said that street magicians are a flighty lot, prone to chasing the next big opportunity without a word to anyone. That Alex had likely run off on some new scheme and would turn up again. I told him Alex wasn't like that, but he wouldn't listen."

Watson tutted in disgust.

Holmes said, "Rest assured, Mrs Meyer, we will apply all our powers to the problem of your missing husband. If there is any trace of him to be found in London, Watson and I shall uncover it."

Relief suffused the young woman's face. "Thank you. I knew coming to you was the right choice. Alex always said that if anyone could make sense of the impossible, it would be the great Sherlock Holmes."

Holmes inclined his head and smiled. "Your husband is a wise man. Now, I should like to see the area where your husband performed his show. Can you take us there now?"

"I can, but I must return home soon. A neighbour is looking after my baby for me, but I don't want to impose upon her kindness for too long."

Holmes stood. "Then we should leave immediately."

Chapter 2

With Mrs Meyer leading the way, Holmes and Watson navigated the labyrinthine alleyways of London's East End. The cobblestones were slick with grime and the air hung heavy with the smell of smoke that curled from the chimneys. Ragged urchins darted past, their bare feet slapping against the damp stones, while women in tattered shawls huddled in doorways chatting with each other.

Mrs Meyer hurried on, her skirts hitched up to avoid the worst of the muck. Her face was pale with worry, but there was a determined set to her jaw as she led the two men deeper into the warren of narrow passages and cramped courtyards.

At last, they emerged into a small, sheltered space, hemmed in on all sides by towering buildings. A makeshift stage had been erected at one end, little more than a raised platform of rough-hewn planks.

Holmes moved forward, looking left and right as he took everything in. He crouched down, long fingers skimming over a few items littering the stage.

"What do you make of it, Holmes?" Watson asked, his own gaze taking in the dingy surroundings.

Holmes straightened, dusting off his hands. "Alas, there isn't much to see, other than bits of debris. But see here, there are fresh scuff marks on the platform, as though someone was dragged across it."

Mrs Meyer let out a choked sob, her hand flying to her mouth. "Oh, Alex," she mumbled, her eyes welling with fresh tears. "What's happened to you, my love?"

Watson moved to her side, offering a comforting hand on her shoulder. "We'll find him, Mrs Meyer. Holmes is the best there is. If anyone can unravel this mystery, it's him."

Holmes moved over to Mrs Meyer and asked, "Where is your husband's trunk, the one he vanished from? And where are the rest of his belongings? I assume your husband has certain tools one would associate with being a magician."

Mrs Meyer wiped her eyes. "His assistant, Jack Turner, brought Alex's items home to me this morning, his cards, his props, that sort of thing. But the trunk is too heavy to be taken back and forth to our house, so he left the trunk with Mr Fitzgerald over there who runs a bottle-making business in that workshop. In return for Alex storing his trunk in the workshop, he lets Mr Fitzgerald's children watch his show for free. Sometimes, he gets them on the stage to help him with a trick. The children love that."

Holmes slowly nodded. "How long has Jack Turner worked with your husband?"

"About a year," Mrs Meyer replied. "It was Jack who told me what had happened to Alex. I wasn't at the performance last night as I didn't have anyone to look after my baby. I stayed up all night waiting for Alex to come home, and when Jack turned up this morning and told me what had happened, I immediately went to the police, and then to you, Mr Holmes."

"So, you only have Mr Turner's account of what happened at the show last night?"

Mrs Meyer gave him a curious look. "Yes, but I have no reason to doubt his words. Jack is a trustworthy young man."

Holmes said, "Why didn't Mr Turner call on your home last night to let you know about your husband's disappearance? He must have known you'd be worried."

Mrs Meyer replied, "Jack said he hadn't wanted to disturb me last night and thought I would have been asleep. He came to my house first thing this morning, though." She glanced towards the workshop. "Perhaps Mr Fitzgerald or his children saw Alex's show yesterday. Shall I ask them? Although, I really should be getting home to my baby soon."

Holmes gave her a kind look. "Why don't you go home now, Mrs Meyer? We can continue our investigation from here. Would you be kind enough to give your address then we can call on you later to let you know what we have discovered. Also, a description of your husband and what he was wearing last night would be most useful."

The young woman gave the details and thanked Holmes and Watson for looking into her husband's disappearance. She took a lingering look at the makeshift stage before hurrying away down the street, her dress billowing out behind her.

Holmes and Watson approached the bottle-maker's workshop, the acrid stench of molten glass and burning coal assaulting their nostrils. Despite the sweltering heat inside the building, a young boy and girl were happily playing a game in the corner.

Mr Fitzgerald, a burly man with a thick, greying beard, looked up from his work, his eyes narrowing suspiciously at the sight of the two well-dressed gentlemen. "What d'you want?" he grunted, wiping his brow with the back of his hand.

"We're here about the magician, Alex Meyer," Holmes said, his voice calm and even. "I understand it's possible your children might have been present for his performance yesterday?"

At the mention of the magician's name, the children's eyes lit up with excitement. They abandoned their play and crowded around Holmes and Watson, their voices rising in a clamour.

"We were there last night! The magician went into the trunk and then disappeared in a puff of smoke!" exclaimed the boy, his face smudged with soot. "Like magic!"

"No, he didn't!" argued his sister, her red hair escaping from its braid. "He was never in the box at all! It was a trick!"

Holmes listened to their conflicting accounts. He crouched down to the children's level, his voice gentle but firm. "Think carefully," he said. "What exactly did you see?"

The children fell silent, their faces scrunched up in thought.

Finally, the boy spoke. "The magician went into the trunk, like he always does. But this time, he didn't come back out. We waited such a long time for him. I peeped into the box when his assistant brought it in here later, and saw ropes and chains, all tangled up."

Holmes nodded, rising to his feet. He turned to Mr Fitzgerald, who had been watching the exchange, and asked, "Did you see anything unusual last night? Any strangers lurking about, or anything out of the ordinary?"

Mr Fitzgerald scratched his beard. "Now that you mention it," he said slowly, "there was that journalist chap. What was his name? Burns, that's it. Samuel Burns."

Holmes said, "I'm aware of who Mr Burns is. Our paths have crossed a few times. What was he doing last night during the performance?"

"Same thing he always does," Fitzgerald said. "Scribbling away in that notebook of his, watching Meyer's every move. He's been coming around for weeks now, writing about the magician's act."

Watson frowned. "But why would a journalist be so interested in a street performer?"

Fitzgerald shrugged. "Beats me. But Burns seemed to think Meyer was something special. Burns was always going on about how clever he was to have found the magician, hidden away in these back alleys. Said his reports in the papers would make Meyer a star and it would all be thanks to him."

Holmes's eyes narrowed. "And how did Burns react when Meyer disappeared?"

Fitzgerald answered, "He was delighted. Couldn't stop grinning from ear to ear. Mumbled something about it making a good story."

Holmes and Watson exchanged a glance.

Holmes asked if they could see the trunk that belonged to Mr Meyer, the one he used in his show.

"Yeah, it's over there," Fitzgerald replied, pointing to the left.

Watson and Holmes examined the trunk finding nothing seemingly untoward on the outside. Once they looked inside, they saw ropes and chains, just as the boy had told them a few minutes ago.

Holmes examined the trunk some more, running his fingers carefully over every part of it. After applying slight pressure to the top part of the back panel, Holmes wasn't surprised to see that it opened outwards, offering a secret exit to whomever was inside. He quietly said to Watson, "This is likely how Mr Meyer left the trunk, but possibly not of his own accord."

Watson said, "Mr Meyer's assistant would know about this secret opening, surely?"

"You'd think so," Holmes replied as he put the lowered panel back in position. "We'll speak to Mr Turner later."

Holmes returned to Fitzgerald, thanked him for his help, and said goodbye.

As they made their way back out into the alleyway, Watson couldn't shake the feeling of unease that had settled in his gut. "What do you make of it, Holmes?" he asked. "Do you think Mr Burns could be involved? I know what that man is like. He'd do anything to get a good story for his paper."

Holmes replied, "Let's head to Fleet Street and find out."

***

The Sherlock Holmes series

Book 1 – SherlockHolmes and The Missing Portrait

Book 2 – Sherlock Holmes and The Haunted Museum

Book 3 – Sherlock Holmes and The Hasty Holiday

Book 4 – Sherlock Holmes and The Baker Street Thefts

Book 5 – Sherlock Holmes and The Lamplighter's Mystery

Book 6 – Sherlock Holmes and The Vanishing Act

Book 7 – Sherlock Holmes and The Cat Burglar

Book 8 – Sherlock Holmes and The Unwanted Client

A note from the author

For as long as I can remember, I have loved reading mystery books. It started with Enid Blyton's Famous Five, and The Secret Seven. As I got older, I progressed to Agatha Christie books, and of course, Sir Arthur Conan Doyle's Sherlock Holmes.

I love the characters of Sherlock Holmes and Dr Watson, and the Victorian era that the stories are set in. It seemed only natural that one day, I would write some of my own Sherlock stories. I love creating new mysteries for Mr Holmes, and his trusty companion, Dr John Watson. It's not just the era itself that seems to ignite ideas within me; it's also the characters who were around at that time, and the lives they led.

This story has been checked for errors, but if you see anything we have missed and you'd like to let us know about them, please email mabel@mabelswift.com

You can hear about my new releases by signing up to my newsletter As a thank you for subscribing, I will send you a free short story: Sherlock Holmes and The Curious Clock.

If you'd like to contact me, you can get in touch via mabel@mabelswift.com I'd be delighted to hear from you.

Best wishes

Mabel

Printed in Great Britain
by Amazon